# DAVEY'S
## Blue-Eyed Frog

# PATRICIA HARRISON EASTON

# DAVEY'S Blue-Eyed Frog

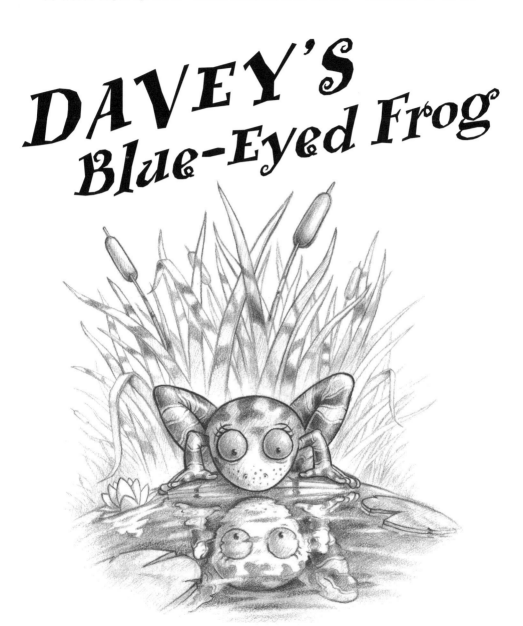

*Illustrated by* MIKE WOHNOUTKA

Clarion Books ✦ New York

Clarion Books
a Houghton Mifflin Company imprint
215 Park Avenue South, New York, NY 10003

The illustrations were executed in pencil.
The text was set in 14-point Arrus.

www.houghtonmifflinbooks.com

Printed in the U.S.A.

*Library of Congress Cataloging-in-Publication Data*

Easton, Patricia Harrison.
Davey's blue-eyed frog / by Patricia Harrison Easton ;
illustrated by Mike Wohnoutka.
p. cm.
Summary: Davey finds a talking frog that claims to be a princess and
plans to take her to school to show off, until he begins to consider
the consequences of his actions.
ISBN 0-618-18185-7 (alk. paper)
[1. Frogs—Fiction. 2. Princesses—Fiction. 3. Conduct of life—Fiction.]
I. Wohnoutka, Mike, ill. II. Title.

PZ7.E13157 Dav 2003      2002010843
[Fic]—dc21

VB 10 9 8 7 6 5 4 3 2

*F*or my friends John Brewer and the late Ed Neill,
who taught me much about friendship and laughter
—P.E.

*F*or my wife, Anna
—M.W.

# DAVEY'S
## Blue-Eyed Frog

# Chapter
# 1

Davey peered into the muddy water. At the edge of the pond swam tadpoles—hundreds of them. He inched forward with his net, ready to scoop them up. But an odd reflection caught his eye. Two shining spheres shimmered on the surface of the murky water, like the reflection of two moons. Davey looked up. It seemed to be a normal spring sky, sunny with puffy clouds. No double moon shone down on him. He peered back at the pond. The reflection was gone.

"Hey, bigfoot, watch where you're walking!"

Davey jumped away from the pond's edge. "Who said that?" He looked into the marsh grass near his foot. An emerald frog with bright-blue eyes glared back.

"That's right," the frog said. "I'm talking to you."

Davey bent for a closer look.

"Didn't your parents teach you it's rude to stare?" the frog said.

"Cool," said Davey. He dove for the frog and caught it as it leaped. "Gotcha!"

"Stop staring and give me a kiss," the frog ordered.

"No way," Davey said.

"I don't like the idea any better than you do. But if you kiss me, I'll turn back into a princess."

Davey thought a moment. He didn't believe in spells and stuff. Of course, he didn't believe in talking frogs, either. And then there had been that reflection, like an omen of weirdness.

"Look, I'm in a hurry here," the frog said. "Spells like this have a time limit, you know. I

have only a few more days to get a kiss, or I'm doomed. So let's get this over with. Pucker up."

"No way. I'm not going to kiss you. I don't kiss girls. I don't care if you *are* disguised as a frog." Davey stuffed the frog into his bait bucket and shut the lid. He looked toward the other side of the pond for his neighbor Becky. She was the biggest know-it-all in the whole third grade. Davey grinned. She would croak when she heard his frog talk.

He found her on the other side of the pond.

"I'll bet I found more tadpoles than you," Becky said.

Davey grinned. "I found something better than tadpoles." He pulled the frog from his bucket.

Becky raised an eyebrow to give him her I-know-everything look. "Davey, a frog is just a grown-up tadpole, and you only have one. I have at least *twelve* tadpoles." She looked in her bucket. "And I'll take very good care of them, too. Remember the last frog you caught? You forgot about it until it died and stank up your room."

The frog trembled in Davey's hand. "Well, I'll take good care of this one. She talks."

Becky put her hands on her hips. "I haven't heard it say anything."

Davey gave the frog a little shake. "Speak!"

"Woof. Woof," Becky said with a laugh.

The frog dangled from Davey's fist. "I'm not kidding, Becky." He jiggled the frog. "Really, she talks."

Becky laughed. "Sure, and I have a tap-dancing turtle."

"She does too talk. But I'll never let *you* hear her." Davey dumped the frog back into his bucket and headed for home.

If his frog had been a prince, he'd have talked. Girls were such a pain.

# Chapter 2

Davey marched across the meadow toward home. He passed the dairy cows in their pasture. Becky caught up with him as he reached the cornfield. Davey kept walking. He turned onto his road.

He was thinking about the kind of display tank he'd fix. People would pay good money to see and hear a talking frog. Sooner or later the frog had to start talking again. After all, she was a girl. Girls couldn't keep their mouths shut for long.

"Davey, slow down," Becky said. "You were kidding, right? You do know there's no such thing as a talking frog, don't you?"

"She's not just a talking frog. She's a princess who was turned into a talking frog."

"Davey, stop it. I *know* you don't believe that."

"Leave me alone," Davey said, walking faster now.

"I can't. You're the only kid my age around here, besides Jennie. All Jennie ever wants to do is watch TV or play with her dolls."

Becky grabbed the handle on his bucket, making him stop. "Come on. Let me see your frog again."

Davey opened the lid.

Before he could stop her, Becky reached in and picked up the frog. She looked at it closely.

"All right," she said. "I admit this is a very cute frog. The blue eyes are kind of strange. But other than that, it's just a frog. I don't hear it talking."

"Give me my frog back."

Becky took a step back. "Speak," she ordered.

"Woof. Woof," the frog said. "Now put me down."

Becky's hand shook. Her red curls trembled on her forehead. The frog fell back into the bucket. Becky slammed the lid. Her face went as white as the frog's belly.

Davey held the bucket tight against his chest. "I told you so."

"How did you do that?" Becky asked.

"Do what?"

"Make it sound like the frog talked."

"She does talk."

"Stop fooling me. You made it sound like the frog was talking. You learned how to throw your voice, like a ventriloquist. Show me how you did it. Please."

"I didn't do anything." Davey pulled the frog out of the bucket. "I'm telling you this frog talks."

"I'm getting tired of this," the frog said. "I order you to kiss me. Now!"

"That was really good, Davey," Becky said.

"It was the frog."

"Davey Brewer, if that frog can talk, I can fly," Becky said.

"Start flapping your wings," the frog said, giggling.

"I heard you laugh, Davey," Becky said. "You've got to teach me how to throw my voice like that."

Davey stuffed his frog back into the bucket. He stomped toward his house. He didn't even look back at Becky. He didn't care what she thought. His frog would amaze the guys at school. He looked toward his house, one of several houses scattered at the edge of the cornfield. No one on this road had ever seen anything like his talking frog. They would know about her soon enough. First he'd show the guys at school, and then the whole town. He'd become famous. Soon the whole state would hear about *Davey and His Talking Frog*. Maybe the whole country.

Becky could laugh all she wanted. For once, Davey knew something she didn't. Frogs could talk. You just had to find the right one.

# Chapter 3

When he got home, Davey hurried into the kitchen. An opera was playing on the radio. Dad hummed along as he stirred the spaghetti sauce. Mom sat in the family room reading the paper. Fluffy, their big gray cat, flopped by Mom's feet.

"Mom! Dad! Wait until you see what I have," Davey said. "I caught a frog, and she talks."

Mom looked up from her paper and smiled.

"Used to catch frogs myself when I was a lad,"

Dad said. He began to sing with the man on the radio.

Kevin, Davey's little brother, grabbed for the bucket with hands covered in yellow finger-paint. "Let me see," he said.

"No, Kevin," Davey said. "Don't touch. I'll show you." Davey took the princess over to the couch and pulled her out of the bucket. Mom, Dad, and Kevin all stared at the frog.

"Speak," Davey ordered.

"Woof," barked Bowser, who sat by Davey's feet. His shaggy tail thumped the ground, as if he was pleased with himself.

"Not you, boy," Davey said, nudging him away. Bowser jumped up and barked again, this time at the frog. Davey held his frog a little closer. "Please," Davey begged the frog. He looked at Mom. "Really, Mom, she talks."

"Oh, Davey," she said. "You have such a grand imagination. Cherish that gift, son." She walked over to him and kissed the top of his head. "Let me see your new friend." She peered closely at the frog. "My goodness. I've never seen a frog with blue eyes before. Isn't it lovely?"

Dad dropped the spaghetti into the pot. He threw his arms wide and hit a low note.

"Remember our talk about responsibility, son?" Dad said. "If you're going to keep the frog, you'll have to make it a proper home."

"And remember to clean its tank. And feed it regularly," Mom said. "No more pets unless you promise."

"Sure. I promise. But a talking frog is not just another pet," Davey said.

Dad grinned. "The boy obviously inherited my sense of humor."

Mom laughed. Kevin did, too, because Kevin always laughed when someone else did.

Davey headed for his room. He took his talking frog with him. He was done being nice. He didn't care if she was a princess. He'd find a way to make her talk.

# Chapter 4

In his room, Davey took the frog from the bucket. He put her on the built-in desk that ran along the wall beside his bed. After dragging his chair over, he sat and then bent over so he was eye to eye with her. "What's the matter with you? You had plenty to say by the pond."

"Like I said, I'm a princess. I don't take orders. I give them. And I order you to kiss me. Now!"

Before Davey could answer, Mom called from

downstairs. "Davey, get cleaned up and then come to dinner."

The frog princess seemed to slump onto her belly. She looked so sad. "Are you missing your parents?" Davey said.

"No, I'm hungry," she snapped. "I don't remember my parents. They died when I was little."

"Who took care of you?"

"*Everyone* takes care of a princess. Soon I would have been queen. But my evil uncle had this spell put on me. One morning I woke to hear his wizard chanting at me. Then with a *crack* and a *whoosh*, I found myself in your pond."

"Good thing I rescued you," Davey said. "All kinds of bad stuff could have happened to you in that pond."

She gave him a dirty look. Davey was amazed. He didn't know frogs could do that. He remembered something she had said at the pond. "What did you mean that you have only a few more days?" he asked.

"That's what I've been trying to tell you. I don't remember the exact words. I do remember the spell was all in rhyme. The final part was about a kiss turning me back into a princess. The very last lines were:

'But wax and wane, but wax and wane,
A croaking frog you will remain.'

I figure the 'wax and wane' part has to be about the cycles of the moon. So that means I have to get a kiss before two cycles of the moon pass. It's already in its second cycle. I haven't much time left."

"But you don't know for sure that's what it means."

"What else could it mean?" she asked. "Oh, I wish I could remember the whole spell."

"How could you forget it? It was pretty important," Davey said.

"Give me a break. I was being turned into a frog. I had more on my mind than memorizing poetry."

"Davey, dinner's on the table," Dad called.

"I've got to go," Davey said.

"What about me?" the frog said. "I'm starving. According to your little girlfriend—"

"She's not my girlfriend."

"That's not the point. The point is, according to her, you don't have a very good record when it comes to feeding creatures in your care. And I can tell you, for sure, I will die if I don't get food soon." She flopped forlornly onto her side.

"Later. I promise," Davey said, as he shoved her back into the bucket. What did talking frogs eat, anyway? He didn't think she'd eat the store-bought food he had for his turtle or salamanders. He bit his lip. He had forgotten to feed his turtle and salamanders, maybe for a couple of days.

He opened the top of his salamander tank. The stink crept into his nose and stuck there. He threw the food pellets in. He slammed the lighted top back into place.

"Right now, Davey!" Mom called again.

"Coming," he answered. He'd feed the turtle and clean both tanks later. Angry grumbling came from the bucket. He'd have to find something to feed his frog princess. And he'd try to find out how many days were left before the new moon.

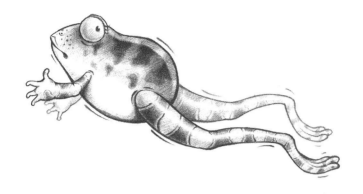

# Chapter
# 5

Davey was still trying to figure out what to feed the frog princess as he cleared the dinner dishes. Maybe he could talk her into a little bit of leftover spaghetti.

On the way back to his room, he slipped into his parents' study. Dad's wall calendar showed the phases of the moon. Davey studied it. Good. He had a week until the new moon.

That left plenty of time to show off his frog before he even had to think about kissing her.

They wouldn't be able to tour the whole state, but they sure could impress the kids at school. He might not be the smartest kid or the most popular. He wasn't the best athlete, either. But he'd be the only one with a talking frog. Maybe he'd make the frog a deal. If she talked when he told her to, he'd turn her back into a princess before the deadline was up. Davey charged toward his room, taking the steps two at a time.

At the top of the stairs he slowed to a swagger. He guessed she'd take his offer. She really didn't have much choice. If she gave him a hard time, he was ready to get tough. No food unless she cooperated.

Inside his room, Davey found the bucket on its side. The lid had rolled off. Puddles of water lay on the carpet. Bowser's big furry head and shoulders were pushed under the bed.

"Bad dog!" Davey said. His heart pounded and his throat squeezed tight. He pulled Bowser away. He checked Bowser's mouth. No sign of frog goo. "Whew," he sighed. He shooed the big dog out of the room.

Davey dropped onto his stomach. He looked under the bed. Kevin's face peered back. Fluffy crouched at his elbow, ready to pounce.

"Bowser knocked the bucket over," Kevin said. "The frog hid, but I found her." Kevin shoved his fist forward. He held the poor frog so tightly, her blue eyes bulged more than usual.

"Give her to me, Kevin," Davey said, taking the frog. "Now, out of my room, and take Fluffy with you."

"Please make her say something, Davey."

"Not now, Kevin. I'll call you when she's ready to talk."

After Kevin left, Davey checked his frog. "Good. You're all right."

"No thanks to you. That dog could have killed me. And that brother of yours . . ."

"Yeah, he's a pain. But he's only four—he doesn't understand. You could have asked him to let go."

"He was squeezing the life out of me. I couldn't talk. Keep him away from me."

Davey's throat tightened again. If she had died, it would have been his fault.

"And if you don't get me food soon," the frog said, "I'm a goner, anyway." She sank onto her belly, looking miserable.

Davey tried not to notice. But his own stomach felt warm and full. He snuck a peek at the frog. She groaned and seemed to sink lower.

He couldn't starve her into talking. She'd been through enough. "What do you eat? I don't have any frog food. I can't get to the pet store until maybe tomorrow."

"In the first place, I am *not* your pet. And I eat insects."

Davey hooted with laughter. "Some diet for a princess."

For a moment the frog simply glared at him. Then she pushed herself high on her front legs. "Listen to me, you barbarian. If you were as hungry as I am, you'd probably find insects pretty tasty."

Davey's full stomach shot quivers of guilt. "Sorry. But it's not like I keep bugs handy in case a frog drops by for dinner."

"I'm sure if you looked around, you could find some for me," the frog said in her bossy tone.

"How about if I take you where you can catch your own?" he said. He grabbed the bucket and put her in it.

"Now, listen to me," she said. "The fattest and juiciest bugs hang around rotting plants. Have you got a compost heap or something?"

Davey nearly gagged. "That's disgusting," he said.

Again the frog gave him her blue-eyed glare.

Davey could feel his cheeks getting hot. "Sorry. . . . We should be able to find some bugs in Mom's garden."

"If I can't persuade you to catch me some, that will have to do," she answered.

He dropped food into his turtle's tank. Then he headed outside with his frog.

Davey let her loose in their backyard garden. He followed as she hopped along slowly, looking for food. Tiny brown bugs flew around some rotted leaves left from last fall. Out shot the frog's tongue. Into her mouth went a bug.

"Cool!" Davey said.

"Ahh!" said the frog. Again and again she flicked her tongue. She hopped around the garden eating every insect in her path.

When she stopped, Davey asked, "Are you done?"

"For now," she said. Her mouth seemed to curve into a smile.

Davey smiled back, glad she was finally in a good mood. Maybe *now* she'd take his deal.

He carried her back to his room. He'd have to get up early and feed her before school. How often did frogs eat, anyway? She'd need a better home than his bait bucket, too. And he'd have to make sure Kevin stayed away from her. Davey guessed she'd keep him pretty busy. But after all, a talking frog was worth a little extra effort.

# Chapter
# 6

Back in his room, Davey took the princess from the bucket and put her on top of his desk.

The frog princess squirmed. "This is too hard," she said. "Lift me onto the bed."

Davey hesitated. His bedspread and blankets spilled off the side of the bed onto the floor. He didn't want to sleep on sheets a frog had hopped all over. Quickly, he threw the bedspread over most of the bed and put her on it.

"You stay right there, and I'll fix you a nice

home." He got a glass aquarium from his closet. "My lizard used to live in this," he said. He set the tank on his desk. He ran downstairs for a gallon of Mom's distilled water.

As he re-entered his room, he heard the frog princess murmur, "Ahh." There she sat, burrowing her froggy butt into his pillow. He rushed to finish the tank. He poured the water into the

tank until it was about four inches deep. He raced back to the closet for the aquarium top.

"You don't need to hurry," she said. "I'm very comfortable. In fact, I'd simply stay here, but my skin would dry out. . . . Of course, you could soak this pillow for me."

Davey hurried to secure a heat lamp to the top of the tank. "There," he said. "How's that?"

"That's your idea of nice?" the frog princess asked.

"What's the matter with it?"

"Don't you think it's a little plain?"

Maybe it did look a bit ordinary, not like the home of a frog princess. Davey again rummaged in his closet. He came back with a tiny, sparkly castle he'd used for some long-gone goldfish. He held it out for the frog to see. "This will make it seem more like home."

"Oh, please," the frog said. "Give me a break."

Davey stuck it in the tank anyway. He liked how it seemed to shimmer. She could just get used to it. He put her in beside it. He turned on the heat lamp. The castle sparkled.

"And what happened to the lizard who used to live here?" she asked.

Davey looked away from her. "He died."

"Great. Well, I heard about the last frog you kidnapped. Did you forget to feed the lizard, too?"

"No." Davey swallowed hard. "I didn't adjust the heat lamp. It got too hot inside the tank."

"Terrific!" she said. "I'm not feeling too secure here, I can tell you."

"I promise I'll be careful. And besides, you can tell me if you're getting too hot."

"Not good enough. Get some rocks. I need to be able to get out of the water sometimes. And build me a cave. Then, if you forget about me, I can protect myself by getting away from the light. And while you're at it, I could use a sunning rock, too, for when I'm cold."

Davey heard a noise behind him. He must have forgotten to close the door. He spun around, ready to order Kevin away. There stood Becky, her eyes big and round. Her mouth hung open.

"Go away!" Davey said.

Becky didn't move. She just kept staring. "She's . . . she's *real*," she stammered. "She . . . she . . . *talks!*"

Davey's heart pounded. All he needed now was bigmouth Becky blabbing to everyone. She'd probably tell them *she* had found the frog. She'd want to be the one to show her off. He forced a laugh. "There is no such thing as a talking frog, Becky," he said. "I'm practicing my ventral . . . ventrillium . . . ventro . . . my voice tricks."

Becky shook her head. She continued to stare, openmouthed. She seemed to be having trouble catching her breath.

"Give it up, Davey," the frog said. "She's not buying it."

# Chapter 7

Becky's face slowly turned back to its normal pink.

"Okay. I'll tell you the whole story," Davey said. "But you have to agree first—this is *my* frog. We're not sharing her."

The frog gave a disgusted sigh. "I most certainly am *not* your frog."

Becky hurried across the room and grabbed Davey's arm. "Okay. Okay. The frog's yours. Just tell me what's happening here."

"Not good enough," Davey said. "Pinky swear." He held up his pinky finger.

Becky hooked her little finger around his. "I swear," she said.

Becky was a pain and a blabbermouth, but she'd never break a pinky swear. "Okay," Davey said, turning to the frog, "tell her your story."

And the frog princess did. "So you see," she concluded, "I'm not really a frog at all. I'm a princess. Now, if you can convince this dolt to give me a kiss, I'll prove it."

"I . . . I . . . don't believe it," Becky said, sinking down on Davey's bed.

"I assure you, this sort of thing is quite common where I come from," the frog princess answered.

Becky stared wide-eyed at the frog a moment. Then she turned to Davey. "I came over here to talk to you," she said. "I mean, you never lie. And you seemed to believe this frog talked, but still. . . . Is this really happening?"

"Believe her, Becky. It's real."

"For Pete's sake, Davey! You have to free her

from this horrible spell. Give her royal highness a kiss."

"My name is Princess Amelia. Becky, I pronounce you my first lady-in-waiting for as long as I'm here. Therefore, you may call me Amy," she said.

"Oh, great!" Davey said.

"What can we do to help you, Amy?" Becky asked.

"Get this dreadful boy to give me a kiss," Amy said. "I'm afraid I'm running out of time."

"Go ahead, Davey. Do it!" Becky ordered, sounding just as bossy as the frog princess.

Davey folded his arms over his chest and turned away from both of them. "We have lots of time. I figured it out. She has until next week. That's the end of the second cycle of our moon."

"No!" Amy said. "I can't wait that long. The timing may not depend on your moon. Where I'm from, the moons are different."

"Moons?" Davey asked. This was getting weirder and weirder. Did this have something to do with the moons he had seen reflected in the pond? Maybe, but he wasn't going to say any-thing. It would only add to the confusion.

"We have two of them. They cycle together, but the cycles are shorter. And time is different. I'm not sure anymore about what the time would be there," she said. She was beginning to sound desperate.

"You're here now, so we have to go by our moon," Davey said.

The frog gave a long, deep sigh. "Come on, help me out here. What's one little kiss going to cost you?"

"Davey, you have to," Becky said. "You can't leave her like this."

Davey spun back toward them. "I . . . don't . . . kiss . . . girls." He leaned toward Becky, glaring. "I don't even *like* girls!"

"Let me have her," Becky said, reaching in and lifting Amy from the tank. "I'll kiss her. Maybe any old kiss will work."

"No, it won't work unless the boy kisses me. Only the kiss of a prince will break the spell," Amy said.

"Oh, no," Becky said. "Davey is not a prince."

Davey snickered. "She's right. I'm not a prince."

Amy sighed. "Believe me, I know. I thought a little flattery might work."

"But in all the stories," Becky said, "only a prince's kiss can break the spell."

"Times have changed," Amy said. "There aren't many princes around anymore. I'm pretty sure any boy will do. Come on, Becky. Take me to someone who won't mind helping me. I have this awful feeling I'm running out of time."

Becky cradled the princess in her arms.

Davey raced to the door and shut it. He stood in front of it. Becky was *not* going out that door with his frog.

# Chapter 8

Becky marched right up to him and shoved her face close to his. "Davey, you have to kiss her."

"Why?" Davey demanded.

"Because I *command* you to kiss me!" Princess Amelia shouted.

Becky bent her head toward Amy. "You might get further if you asked him nicely and said please."

"I am a princess. Princesses do not have to ask

nicely." Princess Amelia gave Davey her blue-eyed glare. "Do it, boy!"

"And I don't take orders from frogs!" Davey said.

"Davey, you have to," Becky said.

Davey put his hands on his hips. "Here's the deal: She goes to school with me tomorrow. She talks when I tell her to, and then I'll kiss her before the end of next week."

"No, you can't take her to school," said Becky. "If people knew about her, she'd never be safe. What if someone stole her? And what if you're wrong about the time? You have to kiss her now—before it's too late."

For a while no one said anything. Davey squared himself and leaned against the door. He wasn't budging on this. The guys wouldn't believe him unless they heard the frog talk. . . . But Becky was right. It might not be safe to show the frog princess to everyone.

"How about this?" he finally said, looking only at Becky. "Tomorrow's Friday. On Saturday, I'll invite some of my friends over. The frog talks when I tell her to. We do a little show. Then on Saturday night, I kiss her. What do you say?"

Becky frowned and shook her head.

The princess puffed herself up. She shook all over and her eyes bulged. "Kiss me now! I am not part of any *show!* I do not perform on command!"

Davey looked at her closely. "Wow! It would be great if you could do that in our show."

The princess let out a loud, long wail. Becky gently stroked her back with one finger.

"Okay. Okay," Becky said. "Saturday, then. But you have to promise, Davey."

"Yeah, sure," Davey answered. "Now let me finish this tank so the frog has somewhere to spend the night."

Davey took Amy from Becky and put her back into the tank. He pushed Becky toward the door.

Outside, Becky helped him gather stones from his mother's rock garden. She quietly piled the rocks in her arms. She didn't talk, and she didn't look at him. Well, he wouldn't talk to her, either. Davey bent to gather more flat river rocks. The biggest thing that had ever happened to him was finding that frog. For once, he felt special. He wasn't going to let Becky ruin it.

Becky started back to the house.

Davey straightened up and watched her go. His stomach quivered as if a million tadpoles swam in it. No matter how annoyed he got with Becky, she never got angry with him. "Becky, wait," he said. "Don't be mad."

Becky turned back to him. Her eyes looked sad, not angry.

Maybe if he explained. Everything was so easy for her—schoolwork, making friends. She was even the star of the soccer team. Maybe she just didn't know what this meant to him. He searched for the right words, but they didn't come. Instead, he said, "Look. I really will keep my promise and kiss her on Saturday. That's plenty of time."

"I know. You always keep your promises."

"Then what's the matter with you? Why aren't you talking to me?"

"I don't know. I just . . . Never mind." Becky started toward the back door and then turned back to him. "What if you're wrong, Davey? What if her time limit is up tonight? What if it's up this very hour? Then she'll be a frog forever."

Davey's chest tightened, and his palms filmed with sweat. No! He had very carefully figured out the timing. He pushed the bad thoughts from his mind. "She gets kissed on Saturday night," he said. "*After* my friends see her." He was sure he was right. He had to be.

# Chapter 9

When they finished the tank, Davey plucked the princess from the water. He deposited her on the sunning ledge. Immediately, she hopped into the rock cave underneath. Davey tapped on the glass of the aquarium. "Hey, come out and talk to us."

The princess did not come out.

"Maybe she wants to sleep," Becky said.

"It's early," Davey said, still tapping on the glass.

"Look. We have our spelling test tomorrow. Let's study our spelling words," Becky said. She walked over to his desk and pulled his spelling book off the pile. She sat cross-legged on the floor and opened the book.

But before they could get started, the phone rang. It was Becky's mother calling her home.

Davey followed her out the bedroom door to the top of the steps. "Remember—she's *my* frog. I get to tell the kids at school tomorrow. Not you."

Becky scowled.

"Well, I guess you could invite some of the girls over to see her on Saturday. But ask me first."

"I don't want any of the girls to come. I don't want anyone to come. Davey, she may look like a frog, but she's a person—a princess person. You need to be nicer to her." Becky walked down the steps without looking back.

When he got to his room again, Davey tapped on the tank. "Hey, Princess. Come out of there and let's talk."

The princess stayed in her cave.

Davey bent over the tank and said more softly, "Come on. I'm trying to be nice."

"Nice?" The frog jumped from her hiding place. "You are irresponsible and uncaring. I don't call that nice."

Davey winced. His cheeks warmed. "I know sometimes I'm a little irresponsible. At least, that's what my parents tell me. But I do care. Really I do."

"No, you don't. If you cared, you'd give me a kiss and break this spell."

"Look, I will help you out. But you have to promise to help me first. The guys from school have to hear you talk."

She hopped onto the sunning rock on top of her cave. She gave him her froggy glare.

Davey turned away. He picked up the spelling book and pretended to study it. He felt the way he had the time he'd caught Fluffy's head in the door. She'd had to stay at the vet's for two days. Of course, then it had been an accident. Davey pushed the bad feelings away. It wasn't like he was going to make her stay a frog forever.

"You can't leave me like this," she said. "I

want to be a princess again. I want to run in the woods. And ride ponies. And play games with my friends," she said.

He looked closely at her. She looked sad. But

he knew what she was doing. She was trying to make him feel sorry for her.

"You know, you might be better off the way you are. I mean, what if I kiss you and you zap back to your world? What will happen to you? Your uncle probably won't be too happy to see you."

The frog swallowed hard and trembled. "Actually, I thought I'd stay here for a while. I could establish my court in this place."

"We don't have princesses or kings or queens here. We have a president. And every four years people vote to decide who that will be," Davey said.

"That seems like a lot of bother. . . . I think you'll like having a princess and a royal court. You could be my page."

"Oh, yeah, that'd be great," Davey said sarcastically. Just what he wanted—to be a servant in his own home. "You might want to consider staying a frog. After all, there are lots of girls around, but you're the only talking frog. I mean, it's sad that this happened to you. Still, it's kind of cool. Now you're one of a kind."

"Cool? You think being a frog is cool? Imagine eating nothing but bugs and worms. And trying to stay away from herons and water snakes. A heron's beak could turn me into a frog kebab. And snakes swallow frogs whole."

Davey felt a shaky feeling in his chest. He didn't like snakes—not at all. Poor frog. "Hey, being a frog is still better than being a girl," he teased, trying to make her laugh.

Without another word the frog princess hopped back into her cave.

"You're not much fun when you pout," Davey said. Now he had another problem. He'd promised to kiss her on Saturday. He guessed once she'd been changed back into a girl his parents would let her stay. But he sure didn't want to live with a princess. Even worse, what if she did zoom back to her own world? What would happen to her? And why did it all make him feel so awful?

# Chapter
# 10

Davey bolted upright in bed. Clammy sweat filmed his back. Behind his breastbone, his heart raced. He'd barely escaped—but he wasn't sure from what. He remembered a lizard, a wizard, and a dinosaur-sized frog. Hundreds of small frogs ran from the dinosaur frog. Somewhere a scared, tiny frog leaped away as hundreds of hands grabbed for her. But the rest of the crazy dream was gone. Pearly dawn leaked around his window shades.

He slipped out of bed and fed the salamanders and his turtle. The turtle's terrarium smelled almost as bad as the salamanders'. After school he'd change their water, for sure.

He opened the lid on the frog's tank. "Time to get up," he said, scooping her off her sunning rock.

"I'm not awake yet," she snapped. "Put me down."

"I have to go to school soon. Breakfast is now or never."

He took her outside and put her down at the edge of the garden.

She hopped onto the woolly toe of his slippers. "This grass is cold and wet, and there won't be any good bugs out yet." But almost immediately her tongue shot out and snagged what looked like a mosquito.

Davey crossed his arms over his chest. She was so ungrateful. If she didn't have him, she'd be dodging water snakes.

Snakes? Last week he'd seen a huge blacksnake in the garden. It had been sunning itself on the big rock.

The snake wasn't there now. But maybe it was hiding behind the rock. "Stay right where you are," Davey said. "Don't move until I come back."

He ran ahead. He crept around the tall plants by the rock, being careful not to get too close. He looked under the bushes. No snake. He looked everywhere a snake might hide. Still no snake. His frog was safe for now.

Davey turned back to her. She was gone.

His knees trembled. Sweat ran down the back of his neck. What had happened to her? He got down on his hands and knees. He crawled in circles, the dew on the grass soaking his pajamas. He looked left and right. He made each circle a little wider. Just ahead of him movement caught his eye. A black shadow winged toward him across the grass. Davey looked up. A crow dive-bombed from the sky.

"Quick! Over here," the frog called.

Davey jumped to his feet. He ran, waving his arms to scare the crow. The crow turned away. Something soft smashed under Davey's foot. He felt it squish out around the rubber sole of

his slipper. "No!" he screamed. He didn't dare look down. He'd saved her from the crow only to kill her with his own big feet.

The tinkling of a tiny giggle caught his ears. At the same time a nasty, but familiar, smell hit his nose. Davey looked down. Dog poop seeped around his slipper.

"Oh, man!" he muttered. "Thanks a lot, Bowser." He tried to rub his slipper clean in the grass.

The frog's laughter got louder and ruder. Davey reached down and snatched her. "Breakfast is over," he said.

She chuckled all the way back to her tank.

"It's not funny," Davey growled.

"What's not funny, Davey?" Kevin asked, coming into the room.

Davey didn't look at his brother. "Right now nothing is funny."

"But I heard you laughing."

Davey almost told him the laughter had been the frog's. But then Kevin would try to make her laugh again. He'd spend the whole day tormenting her. She deserved it, but she might not survive it.

"Okay. I was laughing, but I didn't mean it," Davey said. "Now scram. I have to get dressed for school."

Kevin backed out the door. "Meany," he muttered.

Davey shut the door and glared at the frog. "You're more trouble than you're worth."

She giggled again, a very girly kind of giggle. She could be every bit as annoying as Becky. Davey threw his bathrobe over her tank so she wouldn't be able to see him getting dressed.

Before he left for school, he hung up his robe. He checked the heat lamp and turned it to low. His frog seemed happy enough, sunning herself on a rock. Good. Now he wouldn't worry so much while he was at school. The terrified frog from his dream leaped through his mind.

"Princess Amelia," he said. "Are you scared?"

"Princesses don't get scared," she snapped.

Davey looked closely at her. "You *look* scared."

"All right," she blurted. "I am afraid—afraid of being a frog forever. So I'll do it. I'll perform for your little friends. But you have to kiss me right after. And you'd better be right about my time limit."

"Yes!" Davey said. He gave a jump in the air. Of course he'd stick to his end of the deal. At the thought of kissing her green lips, his stomach flipped. At least he *hoped* he could stick to it.

# Chapter 11

As Davey gathered his books, worry again seeped in. The frog had agreed to perform for his friends, so why was he fretting? He walked back to the tank. The princess still sunned on her rock ledge. She looked kind of cute with her eyes closed and her little nose pointing toward the light. "I need to ask you something."

"Be quick about it," she snapped.

"Aren't you afraid about what will happen when you turn back into a princess?"

"Why should I be afraid? With a few changes I think I'll like it here."

"Yeah, I know," Davey said with a shudder, imagining life as her page. "But what if you can't stay here? What if you fly back to your own world when I kiss you?"

"You will simply have to hold me tightly, so that doesn't happen."

"But maybe I won't be able to. What will happen then?"

"We'll think of something," she said, her voice shrill. "It's not safe for me to go home yet. It may never be."

Davey stuffed his books in his backpack, remembering the fleeing frogs in his dream. "But if you don't go back, what will happen to your kingdom—to your people?"

"I can't worry about them. Not now! I have problems of my own." She hopped into her cave.

"But—" Davey began.

"Enough!" the princess said from inside the cave. "No more of this stupid conversation."

Davey couldn't believe her. She was horribly

bossy. She never said please or thank you. And now this! "Yeah, well," he said, "if you feel that way, maybe your people are better off with your uncle as their king."

He thought he heard a whimper from the rock cave. He stopped and thought a moment. Maybe she did care. Maybe she was just too scared to think about it right now. He'd be scared if he were Princess Amelia. "Hey, listen. I'm sorry. I—"

"Go away!" she commanded.

Davey left and closed the door to his room. He sure had a lot to think about. For certain, he didn't want Bowser or Fluffy prowling around. They were both big enough to knock the top off the tank. But what if Kevin opened the door?

Quickly Davey grabbed a marker and a sheet of paper from his backpack. He printed a sign and taped it to the door. It read, "Stay out! Kevin this means YOU!"

In the kitchen he kissed his mom good-bye. "Listen, keep Kevin out of my room. I left a note, but you know how he is."

"Relax, we'll be out shopping most of the

day," she said, giving him a playful swat as he passed.

When he left the house, though, the dream again crept back into his thoughts. Rough hands grabbed at the little frog. Maybe it wasn't such a good idea to show off the princess.

Another scene crowded out the dream. He imagined himself being slapped on the back by all the guys in his class. He could see them cheering him and his talking frog.

No, he wasn't going to wimp out on this! He'd done a lot for her. She could do a little show for him. Then he'd turn her back into a princess, even if it meant she'd be around to boss him for the rest of his life. After all, a promise was a promise.

# Chapter
# 12

Davey fidgeted in the back seat of the car. Every Friday, Becky's mom drove them to school on her way to help at the soup kitchen. Every Friday, she was on time—but not today. If he was going to ask the guys to come over on Saturday, he needed to get to school early.

In the front seat Becky chattered away to her mother. She only looked over her shoulder at him once in a while. When they finally arrived at school and were on their way up the steps, she grabbed his arm. "So what have you decided to do?"

Davey wanted to snap back and tell her to mind her own business. But still he didn't feel very good when he thought about showing off his princess. So he said, "I don't know."

Becky smiled. "You know you have to kiss her, Davey. You won't leave her a frog. I know you won't."

Davey hung his head. Now he was even more confused about what to do. Inside the school the warning bell rang. Becky took off at a run, and Davey followed. They made it into their classroom just as the final bell rang.

All through announcements Davey fussed about what Becky had said. He needed to let everyone see that he had something really special. But that probably wasn't what was best for Princess Amelia. Davey didn't want to think about that.

But he did. All through school he worried. What if all the kids he invited told someone else? A huge crowd could show up. Maybe someone would try to steal her. Maybe they'd all want to hold her. Could he really keep her safe? What if it was too late to kiss her into being a princess again? But if she did turn back into a princess, then everyone would know she'd been a frog. Man, would she get teased. And what if he couldn't hold her tightly enough? What if she vanished back into her own world? Who would protect her then?

Another worry kept creeping up on him. Every time he thought about kissing her, he gagged. What if he couldn't do it? What if, no matter how hard he tried, he couldn't keep his end of the deal? Then he remembered that Kevin couldn't read the sign he'd put on his door, and he worried a lot more.

The bad feelings just kept swelling, making him feel even worse than when he'd accidentally hurt Fluffy.

After school he raced from the bus stop, not waiting for Becky. When he got home, he charged into the kitchen. Mom was putting away groceries.

"Mom, where's Kevin?"

"We just got home from the store." She looked around. "I guess he went upstairs."

Davey took the stairs two at a time. The door

to his room hung open. Inside, Kevin held the frog in a tight grip. Her eyes bugged out so far they seemed ready to pop off.

"Kevin, no!" Davey yelled.

Kevin jumped and dropped the frog. She landed with a loud "Umph!" Bowser gave a surprised yelp. She lay on her back, deadly still.

"You killed her!" Davey cried.

As he reached for her, the frog flipped over. She leaped under the bed.

"She's not dead," Kevin said. "Make her talk, Davey."

Davey bent to peer under the bed. Fluffy dashed past him. He caught her by her hind feet. "No, Fluffy," he said.

He tucked Fluffy under one arm and grabbed Bowser by the collar. He herded Kevin in front of them and put them all out of his room. Then he slammed the door shut.

Davey hurried back to his frog. He remembered the time Fluffy had caught a baby mouse. He'd never forget the sound of tiny bones crunching. Davey shivered.

"Are you okay?" he asked.

The frog hopped away from him. She said nothing.

"Look, I'm sorry," Davey said. "I put a sign up. But my little brother can't read."

The frog leaped back toward him. "I've had enough of this nonsense!" she shouted. "I can't depend on you. Take me back to where you found me. Maybe someone else will come along. And if not, at least in the pond death will be quick."

The door flew open and in ran Kevin. "I heard her, Davey! I heard her!" He grabbed for the frog. Davey scooped her up before Kevin got to her.

"Make her do it again. No, wait! Let me get my friends. Then they can hear her, too." Kevin headed for the door.

"Kevin, don't be such a dope. That was just me. I was throwing my voice. You know, practic- ing my ven-tril-o-quist's act."

"It didn't sound like you. It sounded like a girl."

"Yeah, well . . . that's part of the trick. Pretty good, huh?"

"You're great, Davey," Kevin said.

"Go and play. I need to practice." Again he led Kevin out of the room and shut the door after him.

Davey sat on his bed. He let out a long breath. He could imagine Kevin showing the frog to his friends. Only two of them lived nearby. Still, they'd both be grabbing at his frog. He could imagine Kevin dropping her, headfirst, onto the driveway.

He shuddered. He could feel the frog's heart beating hard against his hand. "It's okay now," he said. "Don't be scared." He set her on his desk. She stared at him with her sad blue eyes. He didn't know what to say. He had promised to take care of her. He hadn't done a very good job. She was right, and so were his parents—he was irresponsible.

Maybe he should have left her in the pond. Then he thought of the heron's sharp beak and the snake with its mouth opened wide. No, he was glad he'd brought her home.

Then he remembered the crow and Bowser and Fluffy and Kevin. He remembered the soft thud of her hitting the carpet. Was she any safer with him?

Davey looked at her again. Now her eyes were squeezed shut, like she might cry.

"Look. I'm . . . well, I'm sorry I've been so . . ."

"Irresponsible? How about uncaring, stubborn, and rude?"

Davey hung his head. "Yeah. I'm sorry."

"I accept your apology. But there's only one way to show me you really mean it."

Davey nodded. That's just what he intended to do.

# Chapter
# 13

A knock sounded on the door.

"Kevin, I told you to go away," Davey said.

The door opened a crack and Becky's face appeared. "It's me."

"Come on in," Davey said. "I was just about to kiss a frog."

"I knew you would!" Becky charged into the room and gave him a slap on the back.

The thought of kissing those thin, cold, froggy lips brought a shivery lump to his throat. "Before

I do this, we have to figure out a way to make sure she stays here."

"I don't understand," Becky said.

"The princess and I were talking this morning. We've all assumed she'd just stay here after I kiss her. But maybe she'll get zapped back to her kingdom. That could be dangerous," Davey said.

"I know, but it's not safe here, either," Amy said, "at least, not for a frog." She sighed deeply. "I've been thinking about it all day. All my life I've heard stories about my father. He was a great king. Everyone says he was great because he loved his people. So I *can't* stay here. My people probably think I'm dead. But they hate my uncle. There could be civil war. My people need me."

"But it's too dangerous for you to go back now," Davey said. "Maybe later on . . ."

"Davey, no. I've decided. No matter what, I have to go. My advisers are good people. They will help me."

"But what if I kiss you and you're stuck here?" Davey asked.

"Somehow I'll find my way back, even if it takes my whole life."

"And we'll help you," Becky said.

"But . . ." Davey stopped. He didn't really know what it was that he wanted to say. Amy was so brave.

"Princess, aren't you scared?" Becky asked.

"Yes, but that doesn't matter."

Becky grabbed Davey's arm. "Davey, quit making excuses. Kiss her. Now!"

Davey's stomach rumbled. He wasn't sure if his stomach was acting up because the thought of kissing a frog was gross or because he could be sending her back to terrible danger. He held the frog up to his lips, and then had another horrible thought. "What if it's too late and you stay a frog?"

"Davey! Just do it!" Becky said. "It's not too late. It can't be."

"But if it is, Becky, we have to swear to take perfect care of her and not to tell anyone—not ever."

"I won't tell, Davey. But why?" Becky asked.

"Because you can't trust just anyone. Some guys might think it was cool to show off a talking frog."

"Like you," the princess snapped.

Davey looked away from her blue-eyed glare. "I did, but I don't any- more. If everyone found out about you, you could end up in a laboratory. Scientists would do experiments on you."

"Oh, no! Davey, you're right. That would be horrible." Becky held up her pinky. Davey hooked his around hers. "I swear I will never tell a soul," Becky said.

"And I won't, either," Davey said.

Amy made a tiny squeaky sound. It got louder and turned into sobs.

"I don't want to be a frog anymore," she cried.

Davey didn't want her to be a frog anymore, either. He puckered his lips, hoping he wasn't too late to kiss her back into a princess.

# Chapter 14

Davey closed his eyes. He moved his face closer to Princess Amelia. His nose caught a sharp fishy, froggy kind of smell. His stomach flipped, and his throat closed. "Just a minute," Davey said, pulling back. "I'm not ready."

He took a deep breath. His stomach churned like a milk shake in a blender. He tried to imagine himself a prince—a prince who did noble deeds all day long—a prince who never failed to do what was right and good.

"Come on. Let's get this over with." Amy squeezed her eyes shut.

She didn't seem too thrilled with this whole thing, either. Somehow that made Davey feel a little bit better.

Suddenly, the door flew open and in rushed Kevin. His eyes were red and puffy, as if he'd been crying. "I have to see the frog, Davey! I told Momma what happened. She said I should be more careful. She said I could have killed the frog when I dropped her."

"She's fine, Kevin," Becky said. "See?"

Davey held Amelia down where Kevin could get a good look.

Kevin bent for a closer look. Amelia's eyes got big. She seemed to be pulling away from him. Kevin leaned closer. His nose was almost on top of Amelia's head. Amelia shut her eyes.

"The frog doesn't look so good," Kevin said. His voice sounded shaky, like he might start crying. "Maybe someone should give her a kiss, like Momma does when we don't feel good."

Becky giggled. "Your brother was just about to do that."

Davey groaned. Before he could explain, Kevin bent and puckered, as if he planned to kiss Amelia's head.

Davey pulled her back. "No, Kevin," he said. She was, after all, *his* responsibility. He took a deep breath. "I'll do it." He squeezed his eyes shut, puckered his lips, and gave the frog princess a quick kiss on her head.

A bang shook the room. Davey fell against the wall. Becky and Kevin fell backward, too.

A pillar of smoke formed in the middle of the room. The wispy center of the pillar began to swirl. The swirl took the shape of a girl. With a *whoosh,* the smoke was gone. And so was Princess Amelia.

"Wait!" Davey yelled. But she was gone.

He looked at Becky and Kevin. Kevin's face had gone as white as paste. His mouth opened wide.

"No!" Kevin wailed.

"Kevin, it's all right," Becky said.

"No! The frog's gone. And it's my fault." He began to sob.

"Kevin, it's not your fault. She wanted to go," Davey said. "She had to."

Kevin cried harder.

Becky patted his back. "Kevin, I don't think you understand."

Kevin wiped his eyes on his sleeve. "I do, too. She's gone. That means Davey didn't kiss her fast enough. She died and whooshed up to heaven."

"Oh, great," Becky said to Davey. "He'll probably have nightmares for the rest of his life."

Davey could feel Kevin shaking. Davey put an arm around him and gave him a squeeze.

"Kevin, you didn't hurt the frog," Becky said. "I promise."

Kevin stopped wailing. He hiccupped. Tears still streamed down his cheeks.

"Please, Kevin, don't cry," Becky begged.

Davey gave Kevin's back a few pats. After all, Kevin was his brother. He should be the one comforting him, not Becky. "I have a story to tell you."

"And guess what, Kevin?" Becky said, smiling at Davey. "It's a true story, about magic, and you're in it."

Kevin looked at Davey. "Really?"

"Really," Davey said.

Together Davey and Becky told Kevin the story of their frog princess. When they were done, Kevin was smiling.

"So what do we do now, Davey?" Kevin asked.

Davey sighed. There was nothing *to* do. He looked at Amy's empty tank, the best one he'd ever put together. Maybe his turtle could live there. He looked at the turtle, swimming in smelly gray-green water. He never would have let Amy's tank get that dirty. If he had, she'd have had plenty to say about it. Poor turtle. He couldn't speak up for himself.

"Davey," Becky repeated. "What are we going to do?"

"Well, I don't know about you and Kevin, but I'm going to the pond," Davey said, picking up his bait bucket. He walked to his salamander tank. "I think these guys would be a lot happier if I took them home."

"Can I help?" Kevin asked.

"Sure," Davey said. "You can carry the turtle. Get a shoebox out of my closet."

"You can't let them loose," Becky said. "You'll never find a better turtle. And it took you two weeks to catch all those salamanders."

Davey looked at his salamanders swimming in murky, stinky water. He looked at his turtle. It was as big as a baseball cap. He sighed. He really liked the turtle. He took it from its tank and handed it to Kevin. Kevin put the turtle in the shoebox. Amy would never know it. She might not even care. But he was doing this for her.

"Come on," Davey said.

"Are you coming, Becky?" Kevin asked.

Becky sighed. "Yeah, if you'll wait until I get my tadpoles."

On the way to the pond, Becky nudged Davey's arm. "You know, you're really stubborn. And sometimes you can be as rude as the other boys at school. But most of time you're a nice guy, Davey. That's why I stick around."

Davey didn't know what to say. The crack about the boys deserved a comeback. He had plenty he could say about girls. He looked hard at her. He sure hoped she wasn't getting mushy on him.

Becky smacked his shoulder. She crossed her eyes and gave him a goofy grin.

Davey shook his head. Becky was all right for a girl. Amy had been all right, too. He hoped she was safe.

Kevin laughed and tried to make the same face.

Davey forced a smile. The sun shone hot on the top of his head. A warm breeze brushed his face. It was a perfect spring day. But Davey couldn't shake the feeling that something was wrong.

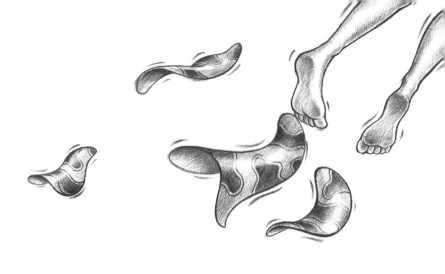

# Chapter
# 15

At the pond, Davey let the salamanders loose. They scurried away so fast, he barely saw them go.

"Please, Davey," Kevin begged. "Can I let the turtle go?"

"Sure. Go ahead." Davey flopped down on the grass. Kevin headed toward the water with the turtle box. Becky stood looking sadly at her tadpoles. Finally, she followed Kevin to the edge of the pond.

"Psst! Psst!"

Davey looked around. Where was that noise coming from?

"Psst! Davey—over here."

Davey spun toward the tall growth of cattails by the water's edge. A girl's face peeked back at him. Wet pumpkin-colored hair dripped from the girl's head. Her eyes were bright blue.

"It's me—Amy. Get me out of here."

"Amy!" Davey jumped to his feet and ran toward her. Becky and Kevin hurried after him.

"Don't come any closer," she ordered. "I don't have any clothes on."

"What happened to you?" Becky asked.

Amy's face wrinkled up as if she might cry. "I went flying through the air. That's when my clothes kind of whooshed off me. Or it might have been the frog skin. I don't know."

Kevin's eyes opened wide and his mouth made a little O. "It really is her, Davey, isn't it?"

Davey nodded. Even if he knew what he wanted to say, he wasn't sure his tight throat would let the words out.

"Get me something to wear," Amy said, her voice rising.

"I'll go," Becky said. "I'll run home and find her some clothes."

"No, let me," Davey said. He wasn't going to wait here with a naked girl.

"Please hurry. I'm cold," Amy ordered.

Wow, Amy had actually said please! Davey took off at a run, not even annoyed that she was still bossing him around. He was out of breath by the time he charged through the kitchen door. The kitchen was empty, and he was glad. He hadn't yet thought of what he was going to tell his parents.

Fluffy skittered away as he ran toward the stairs. Bowser chased him, barking. In his room Davey pulled a pair of jeans from his drawer. They had holes in the knees, but they were the smallest pair he had. He thought they'd fit her. Mom had put some laundry on his bed for him to put away. He grabbed the tie-dyed T-shirt his aunt had bought him at the craft fair. He didn't know what to do about underwear. She'd just have to go without for now.

He raced back down the steps.

Mom stepped into the hall. "My goodness, Davey. What's the hurry?"

"Oh, Mom, it's a long story. I'm bringing home a friend . . . sort of. Well, you're going to like her . . . I think . . ." He kept moving toward the door, hoping Mom would just let him go. "She might have to stay with us for a while." He reached the door and darted through it, leaving his mother with a puzzled look on her face.

He ran as fast as he could to the pond. "Here," he said, handing Becky the clothes. "You help her. Kevin and I will walk over to the other bank. We'll shut our eyes, too."

Davey could hear Becky and Amy whispering. Becky giggled. Didn't she realize that they had a problem—a big problem? Amy needed somewhere to live. Her idea of making his home into her palace and ruling from there just wasn't realistic. Maybe Mom and Dad would let her stay, but he wasn't sure about that.

It wasn't long before Amy called, "Okay. I'm dressed."

Davey turned around. She looked like a regular girl, except her hair was a bit more orange than any he'd seen. She was about his height, but thinner. Freckles dotted her nose and cheeks. She seemed to be a few years older than he and Becky were—maybe ten or eleven.

"Do you think Mom and Dad will let us keep her?" Kevin asked.

Amy's face went pale. "I hadn't thought . . . I

just assumed . . . I never imagined I might not be wanted. I don't have anywhere else to go."

"Sure, Davey's parents will let you stay," Becky said. "They're pretty cool. I mean, heck, all their pets were strays. But you won't be able to order them around, Amy. You'll have to be polite and just be part of the family. You might even have to do chores."

Amy looked thoughtful. "Well, lately I've had plenty of practice in not always getting my way," she said. "Not that I've liked it much. Do you think they'll let me stay, Davey?"

"I don't know. A stray girl's a bit different from a stray animal, especially a girl who was once a frog. What if they don't believe your story? What if they try to find out where you came from?"

Amy's lips pouted. Tears ran down her cheeks.

"For Pete's sake, you weren't such a crybaby when you were a frog," Davey said.

Amy wiped her eyes with the back of her hand. "Give me a break. It's been a rough afternoon."

Davey smiled. This was the old Amy.

"Maybe if we tell your parents it will only be for a little while. There *has* to be a way for me to get back to my world. I just need to find it."

"But what if you can't?" Davey said.

"I have to," Amy said. "No matter how long it takes me, I have to find a way back."

"If you think about it," Becky said, "there must be a connection between your world and ours. After all, you got here, didn't you? But you shouldn't even think about going back."

"I don't understand," Kevin said.

"Me, either, Kev. At least not all of it," Davey said. "Amy, I'll help in any way I can. I don't know if this means anything, but once I saw two moons reflected in this pond. It was the day I found you."

"Where?" Amy asked, excitement in her voice.

"Over here." Davey hurried over to the other side of the stand of cattails. The others followed.

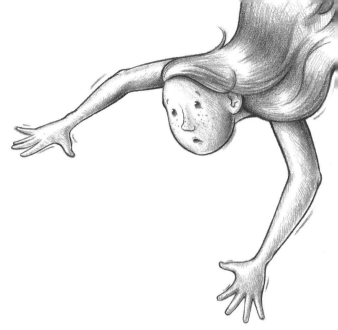

# Chapter 16

Davey pointed to where he'd seen the moons. The glassy surface of the pond reflected only the puffy clouds overhead.

Becky sighed. "Are you *sure* you saw two moons, Davey?"

Davey turned toward Becky and Amy. "Yes, I am."

"Look!" Kevin squealed.

Davey spun back to the pond. The surface had gone flat and black. A little way offshore, two moons gleamed. "I told you," he said.

Amy grabbed his arm. "Those are my moons. I'm sure of it."

"But what does it mean?" Becky asked.

Davey shook his head, bewildered. No one said anything. A white duck skimmed toward them, quacking, no doubt hoping they'd brought stale bread.

As the duck approached the reflected moons, the water began to swirl, slowly at first but then faster and faster. All at once, the duck was sucked into the spiral. Around and around it went, faster and faster. Then, with a *whoosh,* it rose, soaring toward the clouds. In a heartbeat it was gone from sight.

Davey turned to Amy. "That has to be it."

"I know," she answered, trembling.

"You can't—" Davey began.

"I have to," she said. She pulled herself up straight and tall. "Thank you. Thank you all very much. Davey, I know I was lucky you were the one to find me."

Davey swallowed hard and took a deep breath. She was really going. Becky stood with her mouth open, a startled look on her face.

Inching forward, Kevin gripped Davey's arm.

Amy thrust her hand forward, her pinky cocked. "Come on, give me your pinkies."

Davey hooked his pinky around hers. She bent, so Kevin could add his pinky. Becky stepped forward and wrapped her little finger around the others.

"Now, promise you will never forget me," Amy said.

"Never," Davey said.

"Never, me, too," Kevin added.

"Wait a minute," Becky said. "This is crazy. Amy, you can't . . ."

But Amy had already stepped into the pond. She waded toward the reflected moons.

"Stop her, Davey!" Becky yelled, hurrying toward the water.

Davey grabbed Becky's arm. "This may be the only chance she has to get to her home." Just beyond Amy, the reflection of the moons seemed to dim. "Hurry, Amy," Davey called.

Again the water spiraled. Amy ran splashing through the water. The reflection broke into sparkles, swirling silver glitter on the dark surface of the pond. Amy dove toward the shimmering whirlpool. The spiral of water pulled her in and spun her around. At first, she turned slowly. A brilliant smile shone on her face. Then she spun faster and faster, until she became a blur. With a *whoosh,* she rose like a rocket into the sky.

Davey slumped onto the bank. Kevin plopped next to him and snuggled close. Davey put his arm around his little brother's shoulder.

Becky dropped down beside them. "This is just too weird. I don't understand."

"Yeah, I know. I don't, either."

"I do," Kevin said. "It's magic."

"Okay, I accept that part," Becky said, "or at least I'm trying to. But why did she have to go back? She's going into danger."

Davey watched the two moons fade from the surface of the pond. Kevin stood and wandered toward the shore.

Becky nudged Davey's arm. "Answer me, Davey. Why did she have to go?"

"For the same reason I had to kiss her," Davey said.

"That's not a good answer," Becky said.

Davey nodded. "Yes, it is."

Kevin stood close to the water, staring out toward where the whirlpool had been. He leaned far forward.

Davey jumped to his feet. He hurried to pull his little brother back. "Be careful, Kevin. You don't know how to swim." Davey held Kevin's hand tightly. Becky took Kevin's other hand.

"I won't forget our princess," Kevin said. "Not ever!"

Becky nodded. "Me, neither, Kevin. Not ever!"

Davey glanced around. It looked like the same old pond, the same old meadow. But it wasn't. He probably didn't look different, either. But he was. Davey grinned. Still holding Kevin's hand, he headed for home with his brother and his friend.

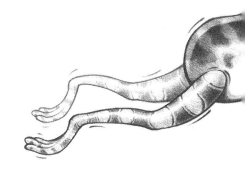

## About the author

PATRICIA EASTON is the author of four children's books, including *Summer's Chance* and *A Week at the Fair: A Country Celebration,* and two novels for adults. She teaches children's book writing at the Institute for Children's Literature and serves as the regional adviser for the Society of Children's Book Writers and Illustrators in western Pennsylvania. She was raised on a farm that overlooked a pond much like the one in *Davey's Blue-Eyed Frog.* The mother of three grown children, she now resides in McMurray, Pennsylvania, with her husband, Richard, who is also a children's book author. This is her first book for Clarion.

## About the illustrator

MIKE WOHNOUTKA has illustrated such picture books as *Johnny Appleseed: My Story* and, for Clarion, *Cowboy Sam and Those Confounded Secrets* by Kitty Griffin and Kathy Combs, which *Publishers Weekly* called "Rootin'-tootin' boot-scootin' fun." Born in Spicer, Minnesota, Mr. Wohnoutka received his B.F.A. in illustration from the Savannah College of Art and Design and later moved to Minneapolis to begin his career in illustration. He now lives there with his wife, Anna. You can visit Mike on his website at www.mikewohnoutka.com.